Little, Brown and Company

Hachette Book Group
237 Park Avenue, New York, NY 10017
Visit our website at www.lb-kids.com

LB kids is an imprint of Little, Brown and Company.
The LB kids name and logo are trademarks of Hachette Book Group, Inc.

The publisher is not responsible for websites (or their content) that are not owned by the publisher.

First Edition: April 2013

ISBN 978-0-316-22487-1

Library of Congress Control Number: 2012947194

10 9 8 7 6 5 4 3 2

CW

Printed in the United States of America

MARVEL
SUPER HERO
SQUAD™

IRON MAN'S
SUPER POWER MIX-UP

by Zachary Rau
illustrated by Guido Guidi

LITTLE, BROWN & COMPANY
LB kids

The Super Hero Squad fights a lot of villains, but the best part of their job is helping people.

Captain America calls in to HQ to report a fire burning on the other side of Super Hero City. "We're going to need the Helicarrier to help put out this blaze," he says. "It's too big for just Thor and me."

"You got it," says Iron Man. "We'll be there as soon as we can! Let's go, team!"

Iron Man presses the start button, but the Helicarrier doesn't move! Iceman and Wolverine peek under a control panel and see that some parts are missing.

"Uh-oh! I forgot. I took the parts for a new gadget," admits Iron Man, holding up one of his crazy inventions. "I should have put them back. Sorry!"

"You forgot?!" asks Iceman. "What do we do now?"

"I have an idea," says Iron Man.

Iron Man takes the Squad outside to see his latest invention. "Okay, this is my new power amplifier," he says. "Since we can't get there by Helicarrier right now, we can make our super powers stronger and then get there fast."

The Squaddies look at one another. Iron Man has had better plans, but there is no time to waste.

"Get close. I will try to get you all at once," says Iron Man, and the heroes squish together. Iron Man closes his eyes and presses the button on his remote. The device sputters and vibrates, shakes and shimmies, and then suddenly a stream of energy shoots out of it and surrounds the Super Hero Squad.

The Squaddies start to feel really strange. Something is not right! Somehow, all their powers are mixed up!

"Hulk not ready," squeaks Hulk as he starts to shrink—just like Ant-Man usually does—down to the size of a bug. "Hulk feels funky!!! Hulk SMASH! SMASH! SMASH!"

The green giant gets smaller and smaller until he is teeny-tiny.

Wolverine feels a chill and rubs his arms to warm up. He sneezes—and snow flies out of his nose!

"What is going on?" he asks as icicles start to form on his nose. "ACHOOO!"

Then Iceman starts to look a little sick himself—he's turning green! And for no reason at all, he feels like throwing a temper tantrum. "Iceman not happy!" he yells.

Falcon's wings have disappeared, and now he has claws coming out of his hands—claws just like Wolverine's!

"I think I could get used to this," Falcon says. "Wolverine, these things are great."

SNIKT! SNIKT! Falcon accidentally slices his own pants and ends up in shorts. "Oops!"

"I don't know how to use these things!" screams Ant-Man, who now has Falcon's wings.

"Iron Man, you'd better fix this. I want my powers back," Ant-Man adds.

Iron Man investigates his newest invention. "Well, that might be a problem. I don't think this will fire again."

"What do we do, then?" asks Falcon. "I mean, someone has to look after this little guy, and we need to get to the fire."

"We can't wait for the effects to wear off," decides
Wolverine. "We have to Hero Up."

"Wolverine, that's exactly what we'll do," says Iron Man.
"You guys go ahead without me. I'll watch Mini-Hulk and
try to get the Helicarrier fixed, and then I'll catch up."

The Super Hero Squad head out, but they have a tough time. Ant-Man is terrible at flying, and nothing Falcon suggests seems to help.

"Angle right, level out. You're going too fast!" screams Falcon. "Stop trying to fly and just fly, birdie...or we're going to crash."

Wolverine isn't doing much better at surfing an ice bridge. Iceman tries to surf behind him, but they keep sliding sideways. "Iceman smash bad ice!" he cries, and demolishes one of the bad bridges.

Ant-Man twists and turns, and then he loses control. "I can't slow down!" he cries before slamming into Wolverine and Iceman. WHAM!

Just before the four heroes all crash into the ground, Wolverine shoots a huge blast of snow out of his hands to cushion the Squaddies' fall.

SPLOOSH!

Moments later, Iron Man receives a distress call. "We can't make it with our powers all switched up like this," reports Wolverine. "You have to fix the Helicarrier to get us there. And you need to do it right now!"

Iron Man needs more time to put the Helicarrier back together— what should he do? Then he gets a great idea: Mini-Hulk can help.

"Hulk, *smash* the parts back into place," says Iron Man, handing Hulk a computer chip. "Put this on top of the green circuit board. Connect it to that wire."

Hulk runs around inside the control panel putting in all the parts with his tiny hands. Finally, it is all fixed!

The Helicarrier jolts back to life and zooms off to pick up the Squad.

The Helicarrier stops just long enough to grab
the other team members and then heads to the fire.
Iron Man knows they are going to have to work as a
team to stop the flames fast.

"Okay, here's the plan, Squaddies," Iron Man tells them. "Captain America and Thor got the people out. Now we have to stop the fire. Wolverine, go blizzard to protect everyone from the heat. With those monster claws, Falcon, you're the demolition crew, and Iceman's job is to clear a path to the source. Ant-Man, you have to guide them in and fan the flames away while Hulk runs in with another hose. Let's stop this fire!"

Wolverine does his best to create a snowstorm around them and protect his fellow Squad members. Falcon tears away chunks of the building and punches a hole through the burning wreckage with incredible speed.

Ant-Man flies in with the tiny Hulk, who is holding a fire hose. The air from Ant-Man's wings keeps the flames off them. They reach a small opening in a wall around the source of the blaze. Hulk runs in and aims the hose right at it.

Water floods the core of the building and puts out the fire!

The heroes quickly finish off the smaller fires outside. Ant-Man and Hulk burst out of the wreckage, sooty but safe. They did it! With a little luck and a lot of teamwork, anything is possible!

Later, Thor, Iron Man, and Captain America put away the fire hoses. "Is everyone back to normal?" asks Captain America.

"Yeah, I built a new thingamajig that reversed the effects," reports Iron Man. "Well, maybe it worked too well on the big green guy. He just keeps getting *bigger*. I have an idea for a new gadget that should take care of that."

"Uh-oh," says Thor. "Maybe you should wait until he's helped us clean up the city!"